This TWO HOOTS book
belongs to

For my two littlest sisters,
Lilac and Freya, the smartest,
bravest and strongest girls I know.

First published 2020 by Two Hoots
This edition published 2020 by Two Hoots
an imprint of Pan Macmillan
The Smithson, 6 Briset Street, London EC1M 5NR
Associated companies throughout the world
www.panmacmillan.com
ISBN: 978-1-5098-8981-5

Text and illustrations © Bethan Woollvin 2020
Moral rights asserted.

Printed in China
The illustrations in this book were painted in gouache on cartridge paper.
Extra monster artwork by Freya Woollvin, age 6.

I CAN CATCH A MONSTER

Bethan Woollvin

TWO HOOTS

Erik, Ivar and their little sister Bo lived in a land of mountains and forests.

Erik and Ivar were hunters, and one day they set off on a quest to catch a monster.

"Please can I come with you? I want to catch a monster too!" begged Bo.

"No, you're far too little. You must stay at home!" Erik sneered.

MONSTER

SPOTTED

Bo went to her room and sulked.

"I'm not too little," she thought to herself.

"I'm smart and brave and strong!"

And so Bo crept out of the castle to hunt down a monster of her own.

Before long she caught a glimpse of
a strange creature.

"I'm Bo the Brave! Beware, you horrid
monster, get ready to be got!" Bo shouted,
as she quickly drew an arrow and aimed.

"Me? A monster? Certainly not!" the creature replied. "I'm the Griffin. Now lower your bow, I mean you no harm!"

Bo was suspicious. The Griffin *looked* like a monster.
"You seem lost. Can I help you find your way?"
he asked politely.

"He is far too helpful to be a monster,"
thought Bo. So she told the Griffin
about her quest.

"I heard the sea is full of monsters!" the Griffin said. And so they set off to find one.

It wasn't long before they
spotted something.

"I'm Bo the Brave.
Beware, you slimy
monster, get ready
to be got!"

Bo stretched out to capture the beast
beneath the waves, but she leaned too
far and toppled overboard.

"Me? A monster? Don't be ridiculous. I am the Kraken!" bellowed the sea creature. "You simply MUST learn to swim," the Kraken added, as she plucked Bo from the waves.

Bo was suspicious. The Kraken *looked* like a monster, and *smelled* like a monster, but a true monster wouldn't have saved her. So Bo told the Kraken about her quest.

"I heard that monsters live in caves!" the Kraken said. And so they set off to find one.

This creature *looked*, and *smelled*,
and *sounded* like a scary monster!

ROAA

But instead of being angry,
it seemed to be crying.

"I'm sorry. I didn't mean to upset you – I thought
you were a monster," said Bo.

"No, I'm just a dragon," a deep voice replied. "And *you* haven't upset me. My poor baby, Smoky, was stolen and I can't find him anywhere!"

"I can help, I'm Bo the Brave! And I think I know where to find him."

So together, Bo and her new friends
swooped off to look for Smoky.

"He must be over there," cried the dragon,
"Smoky always gets fiery when he's scared!"

And so they headed up towards the castle.

As they landed, Bo spotted her brothers. They didn't *look,*
or *smell* or *sound* like monsters . . .

but they were certainly acting like monsters.

"I'm Bo the Brave. Beware, you nasty monsters, get ready to be got!"

And with that Bo threw water down over the flames – *and* her beastly brothers.

"Now let that dragon go!" cried Bo.

"These creatures are kind and friendly. We shouldn't be hunting them," she added sternly.

Erik and Ivar were so relieved
not to have been eaten that
they agreed never to go
monster hunting again.

From then on, Bo loved roaming the land learning about all the amazing creatures she came across – with the help of her brothers, of course.

Because Bo wasn't too little.
She was smart, she was strong . . .

she was Bo the Brave.

From the Author

Bethan Woollvin

I Can Catch a Monster was inspired by my love of folklore and traditional tales.
I wanted to create a magical kingdom full of weird and wonderful monsters.
It was really difficult choosing which beasts to include in the story, but in the end
I settled on three: one from the air, one from the land and one from the sea.

But what about the beasts who didn't make it into this book? I dedicate this
page to those creatures!

The Golden Hind – a gigantic female deer with golden antlers from Greek
mythology. A beast so fast it could outrun an arrow.

Amarok – a very large wolf from Inuit mythology. Unlike other wolves, who hunt
in packs, Amaroks hunt alone.

Hodag – a legendary beast from North America, believed to have had the head
of a frog, the body of a dinosaur, spikes down its back and razor-sharp claws!

Yeti – a large ape-like creature believed to walk the Himalayan mountains.
I even managed to sneak in a little Yeti drawing into this book. Can you find it?

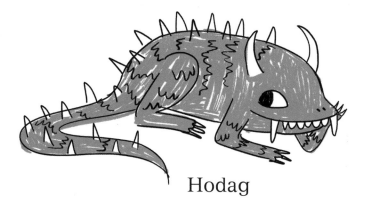

Hodag